DONUT YOU DARE

RAISED AND GLAZED COZY MYSTERIES, BOOK 23

EMMA AINSLEY

SUMMER PRESCOTT BOOKS PUBLISHING

CHAPTER ONE

With one hand absently clutching her throat, Maggie Sharpe watched five people seated behind the table under a covered tent area.

A woman in a hot pink and white striped referee shirt stood off to the side, counting down the time until the contest was over. She wore a large name tag with "Ruthie" written on it in black marker. A massive platter of plain hot dogs in buns sat in front of each of the five people. As the clock wore down, the hot dogs quickly disappeared.

Bite, swallow. Bite, swallow. The three men and two women scarfed the hot dogs down as fast as they could. Some filled their cheeks until they bilged like chipmunks storing acorns in their mouth and then washed it all down with a gulp of water. Others ate so fast that Maggie had no idea how they didn't upchuck the food as fast as they got it down.

At long last, the whistle blew, and the winner was announced. The contestants sat back in their chairs while their partners mopped the sweat off of their foreheads. They were offered a small tray of plain vanilla cake donuts, provided of course by Maggie and Dogwood Donuts.

Earlier that morning, Maggie and her business partner, Ruby Cobb, had carried the trays of donuts into the Dogwood Mountain County Fair for the purpose of providing the donuts as a special treat palate cleanser between contests. Maggie's son, Bradley, had taken over the running of the Dogwood Mountain location while his close friend Zeke Soren ran the Hunter Springs Donut Shop. Bradley helped to fill the gaps while Naomi Gardner and Myra Sawyer Brooks, two of Maggie's most capable employees, operated the donut food truck at the fair itself.

At first, Maggie was excited and even a little honored that the fair board approached her with the idea of providing the buffer between the contests. But now, watching the stacks of hot dogs disappear, she actually felt a little nauseous. She had no idea how anyone would want to eat anything after that.

Maggie had to look away from the competition for a little while. Her eyes and her stomach needed a break from the sight of the competitors stuffing their mouths with food. She looked beyond the competition tent at the rest of the fair, as far of it as she could see. They were at the end of one of the long lines of tents and vendors, far away from the carnival rides in the midway and the food trucks on the far end. She could smell the livestock tent just over the small rise in the fairgrounds, almost happier to smell that than to watch the competition.

Finally, the competition slowed to an end around her. She heard the ten-second countdown and the cheers and jeers after the winner threw her hands high up over her head. Maggie turned in time to offer a new tray of plain donuts to the competitors, their assistants, and the rest of the crew. The winner, a small woman with dark hair, smiled while she slowly nibbled her donut. The other woman and the men sat back merely staring at the donuts. Maggie had to look away from them. Each man appeared ready to lean over and lose the contents of the competition. The woman, a medium-sized redhead, blew slowly out of her mouth. Her face paled. She wiped the sweat from her forehead and rested her head in her hands.

Maggie knew it was time for her to take a break

after that. Just watching those folks eat had taken everything out of her.

CHAPTER TWO

Maggie handed the donut tray off to one of the judge's assistants and walked toward the nearest gate. She stopped once and took a long draw of cold water from one of the water fountains. When she looked up, she spotted her boyfriend, Brett, just over the fence walking around the grassy area outside of the fairgrounds. He waved when he spotted her looking at him.

"You look a little green around the gills," Brett told her when they met up.

"I have to say I never thought this feeling would be part of it when they asked us to provide the snacks between competitions," she admitted.

"Yeah, kind of like I never really thought about

how much walking I would have to do during this fair as the county sheriff," Brett said.

"But you walked around plenty of places as a police chief," Maggie said. "I mean, the city fair is big enough."

Brett shook his head and looked earnestly at her. "No," he said. "You don't understand. There are miles and miles of places to walk here. This fairground is not like the street fair where you just go to one end or the other. This is more like taking a three hundred-acre pasture and cutting circles in it. And then you have to walk around each circle and then the next and then the next. It is never-ending. I wonder if this is what being lost in a corn maze is like."

Maggie wrapped her arms around his middle and squeezed. "But you're as fit as anybody else here that I've seen," she said. "It's not like you're out of shape."

"Maybe not, but I'm still just a handful of years away from fifty, and boy am I feeling it today," he said. He looked around for a moment. "By the way, I think you and I need to have a private talk, far away from any prying eyes." He dropped his arms from her waist and took her hand. They walked about thirty feet to the other side of a square concrete brick shed.

"What do you need to talk to me about?" Maggie asked.

Brett answered by pushing her gently against the outside wall and wrapping his arms around her again. He leaned in, kissed her. And held her there for a long moment.

"Now," he said, pulling back a few inches from her eyes. "Do I make myself clear?" His voice was husky and deep.

"Crystal clear," Maggie said. But the longer she held his gaze the harder she had to fight the fit of giggles erupting in her middle. She bit the inside of her lip, averted her eyes toward the blue sky overhead, and even began tapping her foot against the wall behind her. Finally, she let go and doubled over in laughter.

Brett stood back and gave her room. "Are you quite finished?" he asked when she stood up straight again.

Maggie held her breath, but the annoyed look on his face sent her into another fit.

"You know, a less secure guy could get really intimidated when his girlfriend starts to giggle after he kisses her."

Maggie forced herself to face him. She put her hand out in front of her and waved it. "It's not you," she said. "It isn't that. It's just that you had to pull me all the way over here away from everyone else. And I just had a memory of watching you and Chrissy Farnsworth sneaking over here during the fair our junior year. She looked up at you with her big, dreamy eyes and you..." Maggie cut herself off and began a new round of uncontrollable laughter.

"You really do like to hurt me, don't you?" The side of his mouth twinged a bit. Her giggles were a rare sight and witnessing them almost made them contagious. "I remember biting her lip and watching her start bleeding from where I bit her. And then she ran off and told the entire cheerleading squad that I was some sort of vampire. After that, the girls called me Dracula for the rest of the school year."

"I remember that," Maggie said between giggles. "I also remember someone playing the theme from the old Dracula movie at our prom that year and some girls shouting 'Hey, Drac' at you."

"Yes, thank you for reviving the most painful memory of my entire high school career for me. I love you, too, Maggie."

Maggie smiled. "I know you do, which is why I am laughing so hard because it's just so sweet now," she said. "Back in high school I laughed at you because I felt like it served you right."

"You did? You thought I deserved the mocking shame of the entire cheerleading squad?" He appeared hurt.

"No." Maggie shook her head. "It was just my way of covering up my jealousy that you kissed Chrissy Farnsworth and not me."

"Well, now that we're both well past our junior year, I will kiss you as many times as I can," Brett said. "And Chrissy Farnsworth can go make out with the cows down in the livestock barn." He leaned in and kissed her again, playfully nipping her lip with his teeth.

Maggie swatted his chest and stepped around the corner of the small building. "Oh, I think they're gearing up for another competition," she said. "I'd better get back."

"It's funny how you're a donut shop owner, but here you are dealing with county fair food contests."

"Yeah, I know," Maggie said, once again regretting the fact that she agreed to provide the donuts. She turned to Brett as they walked back to the competition area. "You want to come watch with me for a little while?"

"I really need to head back to the midway," he said. "Believe it or not, I've already broken up three fights this morning alone."

"Maybe it's because of school break? All the kids being around, I mean," Maggie said.

Brett shook his head slowly. "In all three cases, the people were older than we are," he said. "At least the kids have the decency to wait until the sun goes down and it's cooler outside before they start fighting." He walked back toward the main part of the fairgrounds and Maggie headed to the food competition tent. She found her place off to the side again and nodded to the assistant who had taken over for her when she left.

"Up next, we have the competition of all competitions, the last major contest for today," Ruthie, in the pink referee jersey said into the mic. "Traditionally, this competition is saved for the last night of the fair, but due to extenuating circumstances, we will hold judging for The Flame Thrower Competition here and now."

A roar went up from the small crowd. Maggie pulled her paper fair schedule out of her back pocket and checked for the contest called The Flame Thrower but came up with nothing. She folded and stuffed the booklet back into her pocket and watched for the next line of competitors to take to their chairs.

Two more officials wheeled out a small cart. Maggie strained to see what was on the cart, but the trays were covered with large white cloths. Only four competitors sat down at the table in the front, but each had an extra person along who stood behind them. The contestants were all male, and each of the assistants standing behind them were women.

Unlike many of the other contests, Maggie was surprised to see a range of ages and body types. Most of the other competitors were young, thin, and fit. Name placards were placed in front of them as well. Maggie turned to look behind her. The number of onlookers had tripled since the contest was announced. She noted a couple of people hanging around with cameras and press credentials.

Brian, the first competitor on the left, was a younger man in line with the first contestants Maggie had seen. His assistant appeared to be his wife or significant other. She kissed the top of his head sweetly and rubbed his shoulders while he prepared for the upcoming competition. Louis, the man to his right, slowly sipped water while his assistant arranged several towels on the back of his seat. He was a middle aged man with a prominent gut and large spare chin.

Next was Virgil, a man who looked to be in his early sixties. His white hair was trimmed close to his head. His skin was tanned and weathered; he looked more like a rancher than a competitive eater. A much younger woman stood behind him. Maggie wondered if she might be his daughter. She wore her long hair in a cap on top of her head and teased Virgil by tossing a wet towel over his head. He swatted the towel off and pitched it back at her. Maggie chuckled despite her confusion over the interaction.

Neil, the final contestant, bent his head in consultation with his assistant. He was slightly overweight and likely in his middle forties. The brunette woman behind him was around the same age and size. Maggie thought they looked like a couple more likely to ride side by side motorcycles down the open road than participate in a food eating competition.

The next thing she knew, Maggie spotted a large man dressed in a white button up shirt and a bowtie approach Ruthie. She handed the mic over to him with a smile and then retreated to the far side of the tent behind the rest of the crowd.

Another assistant brought the rolling cart to the front and uncovered the tray. With the swoop of her hand, she whipped the cover off of the tray and turned to the crowd. Suddenly it made sense to Maggie. Several trays of peppers in multiple shapes and sizes as well as colors, filled the trays on top.

The Flame Thrower contest was a pepper eating

competition. Maggie decided to switch the plain cake donuts with the vanilla glazed donut holes. She figured the sweeter choice might make for a better break in between the hot peppers.

Maggie leaned against the table behind her and watched with curiosity as the assistants standing behind the contestants donned surgical gloves and moved around the competition table and began piling the first peppers on a platter. They set each platter in front of the contestants and stepped back.

"We will begin with a tame platter of jalapenos," the emcee said. He blew a coach's whistle and the contestants each grabbed a handful of the peppers. Maggie watched in awe as they downed the peppers just as the other contestants had scarfed down the hot dogs. The whistle blew again, and Brian raised his arms above his head. He was the clear winner. His assistant was ready with a large cup of milk and a plate of donut holes.

"Hey, donut lady," Virgil called over to Maggie a few moments later. "Good choice!" He raised a handful of donut holes over his head and popped them in his mouth, all at once.

Maggie raised her hand and waved back, glad her choice to switch to the donut holes was a good one and horrified at the thought of scarfing several jalapenos down at once. She quickly learned that as the competition continued, the heat of the peppers increased.

After a short break, the contestants signaled that they were ready for the next level. Once again, the assistants made their way to the cart and placed another stack of peppers on a new platter and returned to their contestants. Maggie watched as the emcee announced the next round. The whistle blew and the contestants began picking up the long, skinny red peppers by the handful and shoving them into their mouths. By the end of the contest, each one was sweating. They drank long draws of their beverages, filled their mouths with donut holes, and then went back for more to drink.

By the end of the third round, Brian began showing signs of extreme nausea. Maggie watched as his assistant wiped his brow with a white towel. She leaned in and kissed his cheek and whispered a few words in his ear.

By the fourth round, the contestants were eating more slowly. Virgil and Brian swayed back and forth as they started on ghost peppers. Louis closed his eyes as he chewed the peppers as his assistant placed his drink down on the table. He paled as sweat rolled off of his face. Maggie watched in horror as he swayed to his side and promptly lost the contents of his stomach all over the floor.

"Louis, you are disqualified," the emcee announced. The other competitors seemed spurred on by Louis's departure.

When the final peppers were collected and placed on the platters, Maggie noticed Louis and his companion walking among the crowds. They seemed to spot her and head in her direction. "Pardon me, ma'am," Louis said. "Would you have any more donut holes with you? I am willing to pay for them."

"Here," Maggie said. She handed over a dozen and shook her head when he pulled a five-dollar bill out and attempted to hand it to her. "You keep that."

"Well, thank you," his companion said while Louis popped a donut hole in his mouth. "He said those donuts are such an improvement over the bread they normally have."

"I thought the sweetness of the glaze might help," Maggie said.

"It surely did," Louis said between mouthfuls.

"The truth is, I wasn't even sure what the Flame Thrower competition was until they wheeled out the peppers on the cart," Maggie confessed.

"Oh, really," the woman said. "Just wait until this next round."

"What happens during this round?" Maggie said.

"This is one of the hottest peppers on the planet," Louis said. "Donna here will tell you. She used to compete herself."

"You didn't!" Maggie gasped. She was stunned. "What happened?"

"I developed an ulcer, and my doctor told me no more, without a question." Donna laughed.

"I don't know how you all can do it," Maggie said. "I've heard of ghost peppers, but I thought they were the hottest in the world."

Louis and Donna shook their heads at the same time. Louis leaned in and spoke as if he was about to reveal the whereabouts of the legendary Bigfoot. "They won't allow the hottest here," he said. "That would be the Carolina Reaper or a Dragon's Breath, and some contests outlaw it entirely, including this one."

"How hot is the Carolina Reaper?" Maggie asked. She was not a fan of spicy food in general, so the information was fascinating for her.

"Well, they measure the hotness in something called Scoville Heat Units. Now, for reference, the hottest jalapeno pepper is going to be somewhere under ten thousand heat units, okay?" Louis nodded his head as he spoke.

"Okay," Maggie said.

"Those ghost peppers we just had were around one million Scoville Heat Units," Louis continued. "And this final pepper is even higher than that. This is a scorpion pepper, and it is brutal. But those other two I mentioned? They are both over two million heat units."

Maggie shook her head and stared at the platters in front of the contestants. "Why are those peppers cut up instead of whole?" she asked.

"Some folks think it makes it easier if anyone has to go to the emergency room," Donna explained.

"Anyway, these can be pretty awful, too. Those guys aren't going to force as many down as they did with the ghost peppers. Sometimes the competition is decided by ounces. They weigh the platters before the whistle blows."

Maggie watched while the platters were placed on a table top scale and each figure was written down. The remaining contestants concentrated on the peppers in front of them. The emcee raised the whistle up, giving the signal that the competition was about to begin.

Each of the competitors did a version of a deep breathing exercise while the women behind them leaned in and whispered what Maggie figured to be encouraging words. All at once, the whistle blew, and the competition began.

Unlike the other challenges, the peppers were consumed a little at a time. The contestants were allowed to drink both milk and water. Right away, the sweat began to pour off of their faces. "This won't last near as long as the other competitions," Louis leaned in to tell her.

She watched in awe as the competitors continued their slow consumption of the hot peppers. The tent was noticeably quiet. Instead of the constant cheering, the crowd watched with a collectively held breath. Maggie watched as Brian began to sway and pale. She wondered if he would be the first to drop out.

But it was Virgil who grabbed his throat and fell forward. His face landed in the middle of the platter. The emcee blew the whistle. The contest ground to a sudden halt. Out of nowhere, a pair of paramedics appeared and leaped over the chairs and surrounded the competitors' table. Maggie watched in horror as the paramedic pulled Virgil off of the table. Together, they removed the man from his chair and laid him on the ground.

Brett appeared with two deputies and began pushing the crowd back. He glanced over at Maggie. His eyes were round and wild, and he shook his head slightly. Maggie turned to look at the paramedics again. Another team arrived with a gurney and assisted the first two with placing Virgil on it. When they raised him up, Maggie caught sight of his face. His skin was pale and white, but the skin beneath his nose appeared bright red and blistered.

The paramedics began to push the gurney through the tent toward the entrance. One of the paramedics remained on top performing CPR on Virgil as they moved toward the entrance.

"Alright, I need everyone to remain in place," Brett announced to the workers after the gurney was gone.

"We are going to need to talk to a few of you before everyone scatters."

CHAPTER THREE

Maggie sat alone at a picnic table within view of the food competition tent. One of the deputies would be along to speak with her, of this she was sure. Brett had his hands full dealing with the large group of people clamoring around the tent.

Not to mention, given their relationship, Maggie could hardly be questioned by him in public. She was not surprised when Deputy Dennis Barton approached her. "Not the best start to the fair, is it?" Deputy Barton asked. He slid into the seat across from her. "Can you tell me what you saw?"

"The same as everyone else," Maggie said. "Virgil keeled over during the eating contest."

"Was Virgil behaving any differently beforehand?"

Maggie shook her head. "No, not that I saw," she said.

"Would you say Virgil was eating the peppers any differently than the others?" Deputy Barton pressed her.

"No, like I said," she snapped. She calmed herself and sighed. "I've never been to a pepper eating contest before. I saw each of the contestants consume the last peppers differently than the first few rounds."

"How so?" he asked.

"During the other rounds, they ate as much and as fast as they could, but with the last peppers, I think it is called a scorpion pepper or something, it was bit by bit," Maggie explained. "There was no huge rush."

"And all of the contestants were acting the same?" he asked her again.

"Yes, that is what I observed," she said, growing slightly irritated at the repetitive questions.

"And your role here is what?" Deputy Barton asked. Maggie was grateful for the turn in topics.

"My donut shop prepared the palate cleansers served in between each round of competition," she said.

"Just for the hot pepper contest?"

Maggie shook her head. "No, for the entire competition," she said. "I had served plain cake donuts for the first several contests. I switched to glazed donut holes for the pepper contest."

The deputy raised his eyebrows at her. "Was there a reason for the change?"

"Not really, aside from the fact that I decided that the sweetness of the glaze might help with the heat of the peppers," she said.

"And when did you make that switch?" he asked her.

"As soon as I understood what the Flame Thrower contest was all about," Maggie said.

"Did you discuss this change with anyone else?" the deputy asked.

"No, I did not," Maggie said. "I did talk to one of the contestants about it after he was disqualified."

"Who was that?"

"His name was Louis," Maggie said. "He came to ask for more donut holes to snack on after he left the competition."

"Do you know why he was disqualified?"

"He threw up," Maggie said. "That's when the emcee declared that he had been disqualified."

"Where did you prepare the donut holes?"

"At my business," Maggie said. "The kitchen at Dogwood Donuts."

"And the same with the plain donuts you served first?" he asked.

"Yes, the same place," Maggie confirmed.

"Was anything prepared at the food truck here at the fair? The one out on the vendor's row?"

"No, it was all prepared at the main location," she said.

"Okay." Deputy Barton smiled. "That's all for now. You are welcome to leave. Or you can stay around but I have a feeling that it might be a while before the sheriff is available again."

Maggie thanked him and stood up. She walked around the outside of the contest tent and tried to catch Brett's eye. When he looked up, she nodded toward the rest of the fair. Brett nodded back, indicating his understanding that she was about to leave the area. When he smiled slightly at her, Maggie turned to head toward the main part of the fair. She headed straight for the food truck. She needed a cup of coffee and a friendly face.

Thankfully for her, Naomi appeared at the window of the food truck and offered both. "You look terrible," she said when Maggie appeared. "Come on inside and have a seat."

Maggie stepped inside the back door of the food truck. She pulled out a chair from the small bistro set and sat down. "Thank you," she said. Naomi set a fresh cup of coffee in front of her.

"I'm not sure I should have given you that," Naomi replied. "Look at your hands! You are shaking. Maybe you need decaf."

"I just need a moment," Maggie said. She heard more sirens wail in the distance and wondered if something else had happened at the fair.

"What is going on out there?" Naomi asked a few minutes later. She took a seat at the small table across from Maggie when the line outside the donut truck died down.

"Somebody had to be taken away from the food eating contest in an ambulance," Maggie said. "It was terrible."

"Oh, no," Naomi said. "Do you have any idea what happened?"

"Aside from the fact that the contestant slumped over into his platter, I have no idea," she said.

"That's just awful," Naomi covered Maggie's hand with her own.

"Yeah, a deputy asked me a whole lot of questions about the donuts we provided for the contest," she said. "I keep thinking they suspect my donuts caused the guy to keel over or something."

"What do you think we should do?" Naomi asked.

Maggie shook her head. "I don't know. Maybe wait for them to come back and tell us what happened? Maybe go ahead and shut the kitchen down and have it inspected or professionally cleaned or something."

"Why? Did everyone get sick? I mean, if every one of the contestants has suddenly taken ill, I could see that," Naomi said. "But there's no evidence we were at fault in any way here. So maybe, we should just sit back and wait to find out what really happened. It's like that the guy just couldn't hang with all that spice."

Maggie began to speak again but hesitated when her phone buzzed. She took it out of her back pocket and checked. "Brett just texted," she said without looking up. "Virgil Clinton just died."

"Who's that? The contestant?"

"Yeah," Maggie said slowly. "He died on the way to the hospital."

"Did he say what happened?" Naomi asked.

"He didn't say," Maggie said. "But the man died. He died! I can't believe he died from a food eating contest. It's just awful."

"It is," Naomi said. "But it wasn't in any way your fault. You know that don't you?"

Maggie nodded her head. "I appreciate that, but I

think I need to get back to the donut shop right now. Bradley is there and he's going to need to know what is happening," she said. She stood up and hugged her friend.

"I don't think you need to worry about the donut shop," Naomi said.

"Thanks," Maggie said. "But I'm pretty sure the investigation is going to wind up there. I need to go and get him prepared for that."

CHAPTER FOUR

Maggie texted Brett back and told him that she was headed to Dogwood Donuts to check in with Bradley. She was grateful for the man in charge at the Hunter Springs location, Zeke Soren, who was capable enough of keeping things going while her son was at the original location.

She sat inside her car with her phone in her lap for a moment. She considered texting Brett back and asking him if she should shut the donut shop down pending the investigation, but worried that her question would be distracting to him, and maybe a little bit superfluous.

Maggie hated the thought of making things about her, especially where Brett's job was concerned. She wanted to be a support for him, in his job and in his personal life. What she did not want to be was a liability to him.

"Bradley," Maggie said when she walked inside the donut shop kitchen a few moments later. "I need to have a word with you."

"Just a sec, Mom," Bradley said. He rushed around the automatic donut machine.

"What's wrong with you?" Orson Hawley asked her. He stood over her with his normal expression of judgment and fatherly concern, all wrapped up in one tall and lanky old man.

"There was a situation at the county fair just a little while ago," Maggie said. "It happened in the food competition tent while I was right there, but the man died on the way to the hospital."

"Are you okay?" Orson asked her bluntly.

"I think so, it's just a lot to take in right now," Maggie said.

"Well, I, for one, have never understood the appeal of stuffing your mouth full of forty-seven hot dogs and trying to outdo the person next to you," Orson muttered. "For the life of me, I don't understand the point in that."

"I don't get it, either," Bradley added. "Why do that to yourself?"

"Well, now someone is dead because of it," Maggie said, explaining what happened.

"Are they sure that's why he died?" Orson asked. "I mean, just because it happened then doesn't mean that's why he passed away."

"Yeah. It could have been a number of things," Bradley said.

"Whatever it was, the deputy who questioned me asked a lot of questions about the donuts we provided," Maggie said.

"Do you think they are going to want to question the rest of us?" Bradley asked.

"I have no idea," Maggie said. "But I'm concerned that they'll want to shut the kitchen down entirely."

"Why would they do that?" Bradley asked.

"Because if they determined the contestant died because of something he ate, they are going to want to conduct a thorough inspection," Orson said. "And that could take a while."

Maggie excused herself to her office and shut the door. She took a seat at her desk and placed her head in her hands. After a moment, she decided to pick up the phone and call the one person she knew would have some advice. She dialed Ruby and waited for her to answer.

"I was just at the fair looking for you," Ruby said when she answered. "Where are you?"

"At the shop." She sighed. "I guess you heard what happened at the eating contest." Secretly, she hoped she would not have to explain it again.

"I did hear," Ruby said. "I had just come by to check on Naomi in the food truck. Are you okay?"

"I'm not the one who died," Maggie said. She immediately regretted her tone of voice. "I'm sorry. It's been a bad morning."

"Understandable," Ruby said. "That's a lot to go through."

"Should I shut the kitchen down?" Maggie asked. "I mean, the deputy asked me a bunch of questions about the donuts we brought in and where they were prepared."

"I don't think so," Ruby said. "If that becomes a concern, they will let us know immediately. It might seem suspicious that we jumped the gun."

"Do you think I'm weird for asking about it?" Maggie asked suddenly. "I was just wondering about it because, you know, they shut down the food contest and all right then and there."

"I don't think you are weird at all," Ruby said. "But I think you are starting to be a little obsessive about it. You need to get out of there and go do something to get it off of your mind."

"Yeah, but what am I going to do? I can go back to the fair or go and help out at the food truck or just sit down at home," Maggie said.

"Or you could pop over to the Dogwood House and check on the menu for the coming week," Ruby suggested. "I was going to head over there this afternoon myself, but it might do you some good to check in at the old house and see Gretchen. Maybe you ought to stay busy this afternoon. I will see you over at my place this evening."

"You will? Did we have plans and I forgot about them?" Maggie asked.

"No, I just made the plans up myself right now," Ruby said with a laugh. "I'm going to reach out to everyone else and let them know."

"Can I bring anything?"

"Yeah, sure," Ruby said. "Bring a few platters of cut veggies. We're going to have finger foods and something else. I haven't decided what that is just yet."

"Deal," Maggie said. She was grateful for the excuse for a distraction. She headed back out of her office, announced her errand to Orson and Bradley, and then went out to her car. She drove across town and headed up the hill to the familiar, large estate house. She'd grown up playing in the house and spending hours on the front porch with her mystery novels when the house belonged to Great-Aunt Marjorie, the same woman who had gifted her both the small house she lived in and the donut shop.

Gretchen LeClair was the new owner and she'd turned it into a bustling bed and breakfast. The older woman brought her own taste to the house but kept many of the old charms intact as well. Maggie loved retreating to the old house to visit.

She walked up the steps to the back door and waited until Gretchen's handyman, Albert Boudreaux, answered the door. "Hello, Miss Sharpe," he said slowly and moved out of her way to let her in.

"I wanted to chat with Gretchen, if she is available," Maggie said. Albert gestured toward the kitchen and invited her to sit down to wait.

"What can I do for you?" Gretchen said. She moved through the kitchen with more agility than many women half her age.

"I'm here in Ruby's place to talk about the menu for next week," Maggie said.

Gretchen stopped and folded her arms. "You're also here to visit the house, aren't you?" she asked.

"Maybe." Maggie smiled.

"Come on into the sitting room," Gretchen said. She breezed through the house, leaving a cloud of perfume behind her as she moved. "Why don't we have some tea, and you can help me figure out how many boxed lunches I am going to need for next week."

She agreed and followed her through the house. They sat in a small corner with a table between them. Maggie listened as Gretchen chatted about the goings on in her life. She had a full house at the moment, thanks to the county fair. Maggie cringed a bit when Gretchen mentioned the fair. She didn't want to think much about the fair just then.

But her plans were thwarted when the front door swung open, and the clatter of footsteps filled the large room. Maggie and Gretchen looked up suddenly. Four people stood there staring at them. Immediately Maggie recognized two of them from the food competition tent.

"Welcome back," Gretchen said graciously. "Are you all tired of the fair already?"

"What are you doing here?" A young woman stared straight at Maggie.

"Ms. Sharpe is my guest, Amanda," Gretchen said.

"She was at the fair earlier," Amanda said. "She was serving food there."

"I provided the palate cleansers for the food contests," Maggie explained. "There was an incident during one of the contests and someone was taken away to the hospital." She left out the part she already knew about the man dying.

"Yeah, and then my husband died," Amanda said. Maggie felt her jaw drop. This young woman, whom she assumed was a daughter to the older man, was actually his wife.

"I am so sorry to hear that," Gretchen cut in. "Why don't you go and rest in your room while I prepare some tea and bring it to you?"

"Yeah, okay," Amanda said.

"I think I should go," Maggie said quietly.

"You know, I really hope they don't find out it was your donuts that killed him," Amanda called after her. "Because if that is the case, you won't be going anywhere."

"I'll see myself out," Maggie said. She cast a look at the scowling young blonde woman and headed straight for the kitchen. When she reached the door, she let herself out and paused on the porch for a moment. Her heart raced in her chest. She felt the anxiety of the day catching up with her.

She called Ruby the second she got into her car. "The man who died, he and his wife were staying at the Dogwood House. I just met her and…" She rambled on without letting Ruby get a word in. "As soon as she recognized me, she started making veiled threats about how they better not find out that it was my donuts that made him sick."

"Are you serious? She just blurted that out?" Ruby asked.

"She did, in front of Gretchen and everybody," Maggie said. "Are you sure we shouldn't just shut the kitchen down?"

"Why would you do that?" Ruby asked. "As horrible as it sounds, the more people who eat our donuts and are fine, the better it is for us."

"That's terrible," Maggie said. "That makes it sound like we are hoping to use our customers as guinea pigs. And if nobody is hurt, we look good."

"That would be the case if we had doubts that there was something wrong with our food or the kitchen or our staff," Ruby said. "We know there isn't, and so we should continue to act as if we think that way."

Ruby's words began to make sense to her. "You're right," she said. "I see what you're saying."

"Good," Ruby said. "Now here is what you're

going to do. Go home and get a long shower. Get dressed and do your hair so you feel better, and then head out this way. But don't forget the veggies for dinner."

Maggie hung up and drove back home with the music on her car radio turned up loud. She sang her heart out to her favorite older songs, reminiscent of the high school memories she shared with Brett earlier in the day.

The music wasn't part of a plan to reconnect with her past. She merely wanted a distraction until she could get home and step into the shower. As soon as she parked her car, Maggie called the grocery store and placed an order for a delivery in one hour to her front door. The service was new for the store, and she had yet to take much advantage of it, but under the circumstances, it felt like a good plan. The last thing she wanted was another public interaction with anyone who had been at the fair.

CHAPTER FIVE

Maggie dried her hair quickly and checked her phone for any notification that her groceries had been delivered. She had already utilized the store app on her phone to pay for the delivery and add a little more for a tip to the driver. Thankfully, the vegetables were already cut and placed on separate platters. When they arrived, she loaded the bags into her car just before she left for Ruby's house.

Her phone rang while she was driving down the highway toward Ruby's rural farm road. She answered on her car's speaker system without looking at the screen to know who was calling.

"Hello," she asked timidly.

"It's Brett," he said when she answered. "I'm just checking in. Are you headed out to Ruby's?"

"I am, and I was going to call you a little later to see if you'd be able to stop by. But just in case you can't, I might as well tell you that I ran into the woman who was standing behind the deceased man from the food competition today. She is staying at the Dogwood House, and she said a few not-so-nice things to me about my donuts at the competition today."

"What did she say?"

"That I'd better hope it wasn't my food that killed her husband," Maggie said. "She even issued a bit of a veiled threat to me in passing."

"Amanda, right?"

"That's what she said," Maggie told him. "I swear she is maybe twenty-five and not a day over."

"That's strange, but certainly not unheard of," Brett said. "I'll look into her threat."

"I don't think we need to make a very big deal about it," Maggie said. "At least, let's not rock the boat until the waves get too high. I mean, if he were her husband, she would surely be in deep emotional stress. I know I would be."

"You would be what?"

"I would be in a terrible place if something happened to my partner," she said.

"You almost said if something happened to your husband," Brett said.

"Brett, you are in law enforcement," Maggie said. "It's not unheard of that something could happen to you."

"Yeah, but you almost said, 'my husband,'" he teased her.

"Do you think it's appropriate for you to be kidding around about all of this?"

"Are you still thinking about what Amanda said to you?" he asked her.

"No, not as much," Maggie admitted.

"Good. I love you and I will see you in an hour or two," Brett said and ended the phone call.

Maggie smiled as she drove the rest of the way to the farm. When she parked her car and unloaded the groceries from the store delivery, she actually felt better than she had all day.

Ruby greeted her in the kitchen and directed her to set the veggie platters in the fridge. "What are you making?" Maggie asked.

Ruby pointed to the wok on top of her stove. "Fried rice for the steamed buns."

"I've had those before, I think," Maggie said.

"Yes, but have you had them with Missouri raised

angus? I decided to use cabbage and ground beef for these."

"That sounds good," she said and looked over to the other side of the large kitchen. "What's that over there?"

"Oh, just a funnel cake inspired donut I was experimenting with," Ruby said. "Inspired by the fair."

"A funnel cake donut?"

"Yes," Ruby said. "I don't think it will be a permanent item, but the city street fair isn't too far away, and the state fair isn't either. It might be fun to have a fair item on the menu during those times."

"And how do we make these funnel cake donuts?" Maggie crossed the kitchen. She ran her finger along the edge of the first donut. "There is a crispy edge to these."

"I followed the typical funnel cake recipe but tweaked it slightly for my small donut maker here and figured that I could adapt it to the larger ones," Ruby said. "I think we will roll each in powdered sugar and serve them quickly."

"They taste just like a funnel cake," Maggie said. She had torn a donut in two pieces and nibbled on one side.

"That's the plan." Ruby smiled. "Anyway, I

figured we could test them on our friends tonight around the fire after dinner."

"I think that's a very good idea," Maggie said. Her spirits had risen considerably since her visit to the Dogwood House and her interaction with Amanda.

Maggie adjusted the vegetables on the trays and began to mix up a dip for them. Ruby continued to work on the chopped cabbage and carrots for the steamed buns.

"What smells so good?" Orson asked an hour later when he appeared in the kitchen. He carried a grocery sack with two bottles of wine inside.

"I'm making steamed buns for our dinner tonight," Ruby announced.

"Steamed buns?" Orson tipped his head to the side and regarded the two women in front of him.

"They're also called 'bao buns,'" Ruby said. "Have you ever had them?"

"Ruby, my dear, as close as we are, whether or not my buns have ever been steamed is none of your business," Orson said with a face as straight as a stalk of corn.

Ruby stared at him for a moment, not registering the comment. "Orson Hawley," she said at last. "You are an old rascal!" She swatted at his shoulder and rolled her eyes. Maggie watched Orson grin and beam in satisfaction for besting Ruby. He stood taller than normal and walked back out the door to the outside.

Maggie followed with a large wok filled with fried rice. She placed it on the grill next to the kettle of water Ruby was heating up for her steamer. Maggie pushed the wok to the back of the grill and headed for her favorite chair, a white wooden Adirondack chair, in the circle around the bonfire pit. Brett arrived in his muscle car and revved it once before he parked behind her car. He walked casually over to the circle of chairs and sat down next to her.

"You look like you could use a cold one," Orson declared. He stood up and headed straight for the kitchen before Brett could answer.

"How are you?" Ruby asked him. "Everything okay?"

"Yeah," Brett said. He closed his eyes and pinched the bridge of his nose. "It has been a very long day."

"That's what we heard," Orson said, returning from the house. He handed a glass bottle to Brett and took his seat again with a cold bottle of his own. "Have they figured out the cause of death just yet?"

"Yeah, you might say they figured out the cause of death," Brett said. He rolled his eyes and tipped the bottle of beer up.

"What's the matter?" Ruby asked. "You look like you are fit to be tied."

Brett leaned back in the chair and gazed up at the evening sky. "We have a new county coroner, and she is a pill," he said. "Dr. Dana Marsh, board certified, duly appointed, and so full of herself you would swear she wrote every episode of every crime show on television! Fact is, I think she believes that she lives in an episode of the show."

"Did she make any ruling on Virgil's death?" Maggie asked. She was instantly transported back to the scene at the fair.

Brett nodded at her. His face softened slightly when he read the concern on her face. "She issued a preliminary ruling of inconclusive," he said.

"What was the cause of death?" Ruby asked quietly.

"Virgil Clinton died of a severe rupture in his esophagus," Brett said.

"Caused by the hot peppers?" Maggie asked.

"That's what's unclear right now," Brett said. "Dr. Marsh said that the peppers served to him should not have affected him like that. That's why she insists on a thorough investigation."

CHAPTER SIX

Official word came from the coroner first thing in the morning. As sheriff, Brett had the duty of serving the notice to the donut shop in person. He met Maggie in her driveway at five in the morning, before she left for the donut shop.

"She wants the kitchen to be completely inspected before you resume operations," he said.

"I knew it," Maggie said. She stood under the light of the utility light over her garage.

"What about the truck? Hunter Springs?"

Brett shook his head. "It's just the main location. Dana said that there isn't sufficient reason to shut the other two down as well."

"So, she suspects the issue came from the Dogwood Mountain kitchen?"

Brett sighed. "It's more or less a procedural precaution," he said. "She didn't say she suspected the donuts, but that she more or less wanted to eliminate the possibility."

"Fine," Maggie said. She slammed her car door shut and balled her fist. "I guess I can just go back to bed."

Brett smiled and leaned in for a kiss. "Would sleeping in a little while be so bad?" he asked. "I wish I wasn't on duty myself right now."

Maggie smiled despite her irritation. "Go on back to work," she said. "I have to figure out what to do with the rest of my day."

"May I suggest that you stay clear of the Dogwood House and Amanda Clinton? I hate to see you as upset as you were yesterday," Brett said. He straightened up and gazed down at her.

"I have no plans to run into that woman again," Maggie said. "Not if I can help it. But I might be working at the food truck to help out."

"I figured," Brett said. He planted another kiss on her head and walked back to his car.

Maggie turned back to the house and unlocked the door. Since the dinner at Ruby's the night before, she had looked forward to a busy day at work to help clear her head of the images from the food competition. She stood outside for a moment after he had gone and composed a group text to fire off to all of her employees, including the Hunter Springs crew. She wanted to make sure everyone was aware of what was happening in the Dogwood Mountain location.

One she was inside, Maggie kicked off her shoes and undressed. She pulled her yoga pants and a t-shirt on and settled into bed. What else did she have to do? She considered showing up early at the food truck, but she was determined not to make a nuisance of herself with her staff.

Maggie fell back to sleep rather quickly. She was awakened a few minutes after eight by the sound of someone pounding hard on the front door. Maggie roused herself from her bed. She stood up and hesitated while her head caught up with her senses. When she was steady on her feet, she straightened her shirt and her pants and padded out of her room, down the hall and into the living room.

Going back to bed resulted in a deep sleep for her. Maggie was not fully with it when she pulled the front door open and stared at the middle aged woman on the other side.

"Maggie Sharpe," the woman said. Her eyes roved over Maggie from head to toe.

"Yes," Maggie said. "Who are you?"

"Dr. Dana Marsh, Dogwood Mountain County Coroner's office." The woman adjusted her long, wispy kimono cardigan over her shoulders. The dark blue cardigan was spotted with large yellow flowers and stood out compared to the sleek dress pants and off-white short-sleeved silk blouse the woman wore under it.

"What can I do for you, Dr. Marsh?"

"For starters, you can invite me inside out of this wretched humidity before my hair turns into a coiled mess on top of my head," the doctor said. Maggie stepped out of the way and allowed the woman inside of her home. She shut the door behind her and stood for a moment.

"Maybe you could invite me to sit down?"

Maggie nodded and led the way into the living room without a second thought. "Would you like a cup of coffee?" she asked her absently.

"Maybe in a little while," Dr. Marsh said. "First I have a few questions to ask you."

"Okay," Maggie said.

"For one thing, why did you decide to switch the donuts to donut holes at the Flame Thrower competition yesterday?"

"The sweetness," Maggie said quickly. She

rubbed her eyes and stared at the woman. "Do you mind telling me why you're here at my house?"

"Again, I am the new county medical examiner," Dr. Marsh said. "I am here to ask you some questions about the donuts at the county fair food contest yesterday."

"Okay," Maggie said flatly. "But why did you come here? I could have met you somewhere."

"Tell me why you thought the sweetness would be a better choice for the hot pepper contests."

"Because the sweetness would help neutralize the heat of the peppers," Maggie said, realizing her efforts were fruitless. This woman wasn't going anywhere. "At least, that's what I thought would happen."

"And you prepared the donuts in the donut shop in the same manner you have always prepared them? Or did you use a different ingredient? Even the smallest change is important to note," Dr. Marsh said.

Maggie shook her head. "Nothing different at all," she said. "I don't know if there is any proof that the sweetness would help, but it just made sense to me. And one or two of the contestants agreed."

"Okay, and you have no idea who any of those contestants were before you served the donuts."

"I never met any of them," Maggie said. "I don't

think I've ever seen them around town or at either donut shop location."

Dr. Marsh nodded her head. "Are you aware that there is an inspection team going over your donut shop kitchen with a white glove and a microscope right this very minute?" She sat back in her seat and folded her arms.

Maggie's brain began to fire more normally. "I was not aware that it was going on at this exact second, but I'm not shocked by the news," she said. "The sheriff was here early this morning to tell me about the store getting shut down."

"Why would the sheriff make a personal visit to tell you that?"

Maggie smiled. "If you stick around here for a little while, you will understand that the sheriff and I are a couple," she said.

Dr. Marsh smiled with a look of smug satisfaction. "To be completely transparent, I did know that," she said. "I just wanted to see how forthcoming you were about it yourself."

"Is that why you are here, Dr. Marsh?" Maggie asked. "Are you trying to catch me in some sort of mistake so you can find me guilty of something?"

"Is that what you think I am here for?" Dr. Marsh countered.

"I just met you, ma'am," Maggie said dryly. "I have no other experience to draw from."

"You know, I think I would like that cup of coffee now." Dr. Marsh smiled.

"Now you want coffee?"

"Yes, I would. The fact is, I came here to question you myself about the food contest and your donut shop. There are a number of questions I have to ask, and I usually rely on law enforcement to answer those questions, but given your relationship with the sheriff, I thought the most direct route was to ask you for myself. In one form or fashion, I am also a trained law enforcement professional as well. And you clearly do not appear to be attempting to hide anything from me."

Maggie rose from the couch. "Is that why you decided to show up at eight o'clock?"

Dr. Marsh shrugged her shoulders. "I was going to show up at five, but I thought that might be unprofessional," she said. "And let's be honest. This is the Ozarks. Being here so early in the morning might have gotten me shot."

Maggie smiled and headed into the kitchen to start a pot of coffee. She was somewhat frustrated by the woman's unannounced visit, but she was glad that it was over and done with. "You are welcome to come in here and wait with me, if you like," she called out.

"I don't mind if I do," Dr. Marsh said. "I hear a lot of good things about your donut shops."

"That's good to know," Maggie said. "Have you been to the food truck?"

"I have." Dr. Marsh smiled. "I met the handsome young man running it, too."

Maggie smiled again. "The young blond man?"

Dr. Marsh grinned. "I might be older now, but I can still appreciate a nice looking man when I see one," she said.

Maggie reached for a pair of coffee mugs from the cabinet above her. "His name is Bradley," she said.

"And if you think he is cute now, you should have seen him around the age of three. He liked to wear his pants on top of his head."

"Oh, no." Dr. Marsh looked horrified. "That's your son, isn't it?"

Maggie chuckled and poured the first cup. "Bradley Sharpe, one and the same," she said and handed the cup over to her. "But don't worry. That goes down better than hearing it from one of my employees."

"I am deeply sorry if I sounded inappropriate," Dr. Marsh said. "A little trivia about me? I am terrible at social situations. That's one reason I decided to take a more rural position. It suits me much better than a larger, more populated area."

"Where were you before?" Maggie asked her. She was keen to change the subject, but also genuinely interested.

"Denver," Dr. Marsh said. "You would think the beauty of the state would make up for the higher population density, but it did not. I like this much better."

"Good." Maggie raised her coffee mug. "To the low population density of these hills."

"To fewer people." Dr. Marsh clinked her cup against Maggie's and took another long sip. "Good coffee, by the way."

CHAPTER SEVEN

Maggie rushed to get dressed again after the county medical examiner left. Dr. Marsh informed her that the results of the inspection at the donut shop would be known within the next twenty-four hours. Maggie wondered if that meant they could be shut down for another full day.

She headed to the fairgrounds right after, keeping to the far side, near the midway and vendors' row where the donut truck was parked among the other food trucks. She approached the food truck and waved at Naomi who was there helping out.

"Where is Bradley?" Maggie asked when she entered through the back door of the truck.

"We ran him off for a little while," Naomi said.

She kept her back turned toward Maggie while she waited on more customers at the window.

"Who else is here?" Maggie asked.

"Myra went after more ice," Naomi announced. "We have had a lot of requests for iced coffee drinks. She met up with Brooks and Lexi a few minutes ago and is supposed to be bringing the ice back when she returns."

Maggie tied an apron around her back and went to work filling orders for Naomi. She enjoyed the chance to work in the background. They worked through a line of about thirty customers before they had the chance to stop and rest for a while.

"Any word on the inspection?" Naomi asked her.

"No, but the coroner came to my house this morning while it was going on," Maggie said. "She had some questions for me and decided to ask them herself instead of going through other law enforcement."

"What was she like?" Naomi asked. She had been present the night before when Brett expressed his dislike of the woman.

"Very abrasive at first," Maggie said. "But she kind of grows on you after a while. She made a big deal about how cute the young blond man was from the food truck."

"Oh, boy." Naomi laughed. "How red faced was she when she learned that the blond guy was your son?"

"Oh, very red, and I think that helped bring her back down to earth a little bit," Maggie said. "She said that she took the job here because she was tired of places with a lot of people. I think she has some social anxiety issues."

"Here comes another line," Naomi warned. She rose from her seat and headed to the serving window. Maggie rose, too. She placed her empty coffee cup in the trash and began filling orders once again.

Myra appeared half an hour later. Maggie helped move the ice into the freezer and chatted with her for a few minutes before she decided to take a break herself. Bradley texted her that he was on the way back to the food truck. Maggie decided that three people inside the food truck was a lot, and four was too many.

She stood outside of the donut truck for a moment and scanned the crowd. She pulled out her phone and sent a text to Brett. "Hey, are you at the fairgrounds?" she wrote.

"On my way there right now," he replied. "By the way, Barton is driving. I am not texting and driving right now."

"Good to know," she replied. "Can you meet up with me for a bit?"

"Sure," Brett responded. "Meet me in front of the Ferris wheel?"

"How romantic," Maggie teased. "And yes. I will meet you there in ten minutes." She replaced her phone in her pocket and began walking toward the midway. The heat of the day had not hit just yet and Maggie was grateful for a break in the humidity. She enjoyed the fair, despite the unfortunate events from the day before. When she walked with her back to the food competition area, she could easily forget what had happened there the day before.

But when she tried hard to put it completely out of her mind, the image of Virgil Clinton doubled over with his head in a pile of hot peppers haunted her. She tried to force herself to think of one hundred things other than the Flame Thrower competition.

Brett leaned against the fence outside of the ride and scanned the crowd. Maggie approached him with a wave. He smiled when he spotted her and greeted her with a hug, as if they had not seen each other just a few hours before.

"Thanks for taking the time to see me," Maggie said lazily into his ear.

"I actually needed to see you anyway," Brett said. He held her out in front of him at arm's length.

"What is it?" Maggie asked. She pulled away from him just a little bit.

"Don't do that," Brett whispered. He dropped his eyes and lost the official "sheriff look" for a moment.

"Don't do what?" Maggie asked him.

"Don't pull away from me when you are worried or upset or scared," Brett half whispered. "Please?"

"Okay," Maggie said. She pushed against him again and rested her head briefly on his chest. "What's going on, then?"

"Well," Brett said slowly. "I heard from Dr. Dana Marsh herself that she does not think the donut shop, or you, were in any way culpable in the death of Virgil Clinton."

"That's good news," Maggie said. She stepped back and smiled up at him. "Does this mean we can reopen our doors tomorrow?"

Brett sighed. "Probably not until the day after," he said. "There are some formalities to deal with, but the inspection was nearly perfect, according to the good doctor."

"I don't know if I have ever heard a coroner referred to as that," she said. "And she isn't terrible.

She was actually halfway human before she left my house this morning."

"What was she like before that?"

Maggie wrinkled her nose and shook her head. "I was not a fan," she said. "Anyway, is that all of the news you had?"

Brett frowned and shook his head again. "She declared the death a homicide," he said. "Turns out that there was more than just the scorpion pepper that was supposed to be there. She thinks someone deliberately set him up."

"What about the other contestants? I mean, I saw them each go to the food cart and bring back a platter," she said. "It appeared to be entirely random. I don't know how someone could have poisoned him."

"Well, we will find out more when the tests on the peppers are finished," Brett said. "The lab tests are not complete just yet, but the early tests show that there was more than just one type of pepper on that cart."

Maggie shook her head. "I can't get over that," she said. "The peppers all looked the same to me, not that I stood there and studied them or anything."

"Well, whatever happened, Dr. Marsh told me that the concentrated heat level was bad enough to burn a hole in the poor man's esophagus," he said. "He basically aspirated on the peppers right there on the table."

Maggie closed her eyes and shook her head. "I can't think about that anymore," she whispered. "I think the image of that is going to haunt my sleep for the rest of my life."

Brett hugged her again and answered a call on his cell phone. He gestured toward the roller coaster and waved goodbye. Maggie turned on her heels and headed back toward the food truck. She tried to take in the information Brett had just given her. It was a lot to digest. Virgil Clinton's death had not been an accident or a fluke of nature. Beyond that, he may or may not have been the intended target. She thought as she walked about how any one of the contestants might have been the target.

Maybe the person who messed with the pepper platters had only meant to burn someone's throat or throw them out of the competition. Maybe it was an act of sabotage gone wrong and was never intended to be an act of murder.

Louis and Donna! How convenient was it that Louis had been disqualified right before that happened? Was his sudden disqualification part of a broader plan? Maggie tried to think back to the interaction with the pair just before the final round of the

Flame Thrower competition. Both were complimentary about her choice of switching to the donut holes for the hot pepper competition.

In fact, Louis requested more. He did not seem overly upset about being disqualified, either. Was there something that she was missing?

CHAPTER EIGHT

Maggie headed through the fairgrounds and exited through the front entrance gate. She pulled out her phone on her way back to her car and called Ruby. "Did I wake you up?" she asked when her friend answered.

"Of course not," Ruby said. "Do we have any news on the reopening of the donut shop?"

"Not officially, but we passed the inspection," Maggie said. "It may be another day before the paperwork is complete and we can reopen."

Ruby sighed. "Nothing moves quite as slowly as bureaucracy," she said. "I'm happy to hear about the inspection, but I never had any doubts anyway."

"Yeah, me either," Maggie said. "The only thing

that worried me was the possibility of something beyond our control happening without our awareness."

"Yeah, but it didn't, and now we can move on," Ruby said. She waited a moment, and then spoke again. "Only, you aren't ready to move on, are you? What are you thinking about?"

"I am ready to move on," Maggie said. "I want to get life back to normal."

"But?"

"But I keep thinking about the couple that came up to me right before the last competition," Maggie said.

"What about them?"

"I'm just thinking how the man, Louis, was disqualified right before then," Maggie said.

"Why was he disqualified?"

"He threw up during the previous competition," Maggie said.

"Okay, right," Ruby said. "You know, I have all of my farm chores finished for the morning. I think I'll head into town for some coffee."

"Coffee? Where do you want to get some coffee?"

"I was thinking about a food truck at the fair," Ruby said. "Why don't I meet you at your house and we can go there together?"

"You want to go back to the fair?"

"I think that's as good of a place as any to go, don't you?" Ruby said.

Maggie kept to herself how little ambition she had to head back to the fairgrounds when she had just left there, but she agreed to go with Ruby. She puttered around her house until she heard the sound of Ruby's pickup truck pulling into the driveway behind her house.

"Ready to go?" Ruby asked when she opened her back door.

"Sure, I suppose," Maggie said.

"You aren't too happy to head back to the fair, are you?" Ruby asked.

Maggie shook her head. "Not really. I never want to see what I witnessed at the food competition again," she said. "But I also don't want to go stir crazy sitting at home waiting for something to happen. I figured out this morning that hanging around the food truck isn't the way to go, either. I was just getting in the way of our people doing what they know how to do."

Ruby backed out of the driveway and pulled her truck down the road. She stopped when she reached the stop sign and turned to Maggie. "I have a better idea," she said. "Let's go grab a late breakfast at

Flo's, and then we'll pay our old friend Gretchen a visit."

"You want to go by the Dogwood House? What reason would we have for going by?" Maggie asked. She knew what Brett had warned her about and she knew how she'd replied, but something stopped her from telling Ruby it was a bad idea.

"Do we have to have a reason? After all, she is a friend to both of us," Ruby said.

Maggie smiled and nodded her head. Ruby turned right and headed into the donut shop parking lot. Despite knowing full well that the donut shop was shut down, Maggie was struck by the emptiness of the parking lot. Flo Johnson's car was parked next to her food truck on the far end of the large parking lot beneath the donut shop sign, where it had been parked since she opened it. The Diner was Maggie's favorite place to go for a fast breakfast or lunch when she was tired of donuts.

They sat outside and sipped their coffee. Flo appeared a few minutes later with two plates of eggs, bacon, and hash browns.

"Any idea when the donut shop is going to reopen?" Flo asked when she handed over their plates. "You wouldn't believe how many folks have come up here today just to ask me about that."

"I'm sorry about that," Maggie said. "I think we will be back in business the day after tomorrow."

"I sure hope so," Flo said. She smiled and winked at the two of them. "Let's be honest. More than half of my sales are from folks who also eat donuts each morning. I don't think I could keep the doors open if I wasn't parked here."

"Oh, I don't think that's true," Ruby said. "You run a tight ship. I think you could handle it on your own."

Flo rested a tray against her hip. "I don't think I want to put that to the test, so get those doors open again," she said over her shoulder as she walked back inside her food truck.

Maggie shared a smile with Ruby. Flo's good-natured jab helped lift her spirits a bit.

"So," Ruby began. "Tell me a little bit about this couple from the food competition. Louis and Donna were their names?"

Maggie bit off a piece of bacon and nodded her head. "That's right, although I don't think I caught last names," she said. "I think they were a couple. They were at least companions."

"Were they newbies or hobbyists?" Ruby asked.

Maggie shook her head. "Hobbyists or more," she said. "In fact, Louis said that Donna used to compete, but she had to quit because she developed an ulcer, and her doctor told her no more."

Ruby wagged her head side to side. "That could pass the sniff test as a motive," she said. "But you wouldn't think she would still hang around as a groupie."

"They call themselves 'assistants,'" Maggie said. "They are the ones who get the food for the contestant and help with water or whatever."

"Even so, I think it would be hard to hang around the sport you were forced to leave if you were bitter enough to sabotage it," Ruby said.

"But they did seem pretty okay with the fact that Louis was disqualified. And it sure did seem like the hot pepper contest was the biggest part of the entire competition," Maggie said. "Could it be that they were putting on an act, so it didn't seem like they were that upset?"

"Hold on a minute," Ruby said. She pointed her fork in Maggie's direction. "Think about what you are saying here. If they were putting on an act to cover up being upset, would they have had the time to sabotage the peppers? It would have taken far more planning than that."

Maggie nodded slowly. "Unless the act was part

of a bigger scheme," she said. "But that means that they would have had to throw the contest right before that."

"As in, Louis threw up on purpose just to be disqualified?"

Maggie nodded. "That's how they would have had to do it," she said. "Otherwise, they would have been right there when Virgil died."

"Did they approach the food cart with the peppers on it? Or did they get close enough to alter it in any way?"

"Not that I saw, no," Maggie said. "Aside from the fact that they simply were not at the contest table at the time of Virgil's death, I don't think anything else would have changed in terms of the way the contest ran."

"In order for them to be responsible for his death, they would have had to have access to the peppers long before the competition," Ruby said. "I mean, I don't know where the peppers were the entire time the rest of the contest was happening, but a lot of factors would have to be in place for someone to poison an entire platter."

"Hold on a minute, though," Maggie said. "They would have to have not only accessed the peppers without another soul observing them, they would have also had to poison only the peppers that would be served to Virgil."

Ruby nodded slowly. "You just hit on something," she said. "And I don't think the county coroner has even realized it yet."

Maggie stood up suddenly and gathered her trash. She walked to the food truck and handed her coffee cup back to Flo.

"Are you okay?" Flo asked her.

Maggie shook her head slightly and laughed. "Yeah, sorry. I was a little lost in thought," she said. "Thank you for breakfast."

"Are you ready to go, then?" Ruby asked her, standing next to her seat.

"I think so," she said. "But first, we need to get in touch with Brett. I don't know if he has figured it out yet, but I'm not so sure it was the peppers that killed Virgil."

"Is everything okay?" Brett asked her when she stood outside Ruby's truck a few minutes later.

"Everything is fine," Maggie said. "But I just thought about something that might be helpful. I don't think the peppers were what killed Virgil."

"But the medical examiner said that it was a hole in the esophagus," Brett said.

"I'm not saying that she was wrong," Maggie said. "But I am raising the question, could there have been something else that caused the rupture?"

CHAPTER NINE

"You ready to stop by the Dogwood House and check in on Gretchen?" Ruby asked.

"I was just there yesterday," Maggie said, trying to casually talk her out of it. She wasn't sure taking the risk and seeing Amanda was a good idea, even if the donut shop passed inspection.

"Yes, I know," Ruby said. "But we ought to check in and make sure the bed and breakfast is doing alright without the daily donut and coffee delivery."

Maggie realized that was the right thing to do, although they could have called instead. "Okay. We should also inform her that it will be another day before we can resume our deliveries."

Ruby agreed and headed toward the far side of

town where the bed and breakfast was located. They pulled into the driveway and headed to the back door. Albert was seated on the back porch.

"Good morning, ladies," Albert said.

"Good morning," Ruby replied.

"Is Gretchen available?" Maggie asked him. "We were hoping to update her on the state of the donut shop inspection."

Albert nodded his head. "I will see if she is able to receive guests right now," he said.

"Is she well?" Ruby asked.

Albert nodded. He looked nervously toward the house. "There was a disagreement among the guests this morning."

"A disagreement? Is she in any danger?" Maggie asked.

Albert shook his head. "I don't think so, but maybe you could return in an hour or so," he said. "I think things will be better after a little while."

Maggie followed Ruby back to the truck. After they climbed inside, Ruby started the engine and slowly backed out onto the road and headed back toward Dogwood Mountain. "Where to now?" she asked.

"I think we need to go where you don't want to go," Ruby said.

"The fairgrounds," Maggie said. "I think that's where we need to go as well. Are you thinking about finding out more about the contest?"

Ruby nodded. "That's what I was thinking about," she said. "I would like to see the kitchen or wherever it is that the eating competition foods were prepared."

"I can show you right where the eating contest was held," Maggie said. "But I don't know where the food preparation area might have been located."

"That's okay," Ruby said. "We can simply ask questions when we get there."

"Sounds like a plan to me," Maggie said. She sat back while Ruby drove to the fairgrounds. They entered the front gate and headed for the food truck. Maggie looked around as they made their way through, hoping to spot anyone she might recognize.

When the donut truck was in sight, Maggie stopped and gripped Ruby by the arm. "Over there," she said, pointing at another food truck. "The woman in line there in front of the lemonade truck looks like the first emcee from the food competition."

"The woman in the purple top?" Ruby asked.

"Yes, that's her," Maggie confirmed.

"Do you want me to go with you?" Ruby asked, assuming that Maggie intended to approach the woman.

"Maybe just walk a little behind me so you can hear what she has to say," Maggie suggested. "I don't want her to feel attacked."

"Good plan," Ruby agreed. "No doubt she has had her share of confrontations and questions in the past couple days."

Maggie walked a few steps ahead of Ruby. She eased herself in line at the lemonade truck and pretended to gaze up at the menu. Ruthie, the original emcee, placed her order and stepped to the side of the food truck to wait.

Maggie stepped out of line and smiled at her. "Aren't you Ruthie?" she asked.

Ruthie frowned immediately. "Who's asking?" After studying Maggie's face for a second, she pointed her finger at her. "Wait. I know you. You were at the eating contest, weren't you? You're the donut lady."

Maggie nodded her head slowly. "I am the donut lady. Maggie Sharpe is my name," she said and extended her hand to the woman. Ruthie shook her hand limply.

"What are you doing here?" Ruthie said. "I'm surprised you came back to the fair."

"Well, I have a food truck across the way,"

Maggie said. She pointed in the direction. "I'm afraid business goes on."

"Yeah? Did they put you through the wringer, too?"

Maggie nodded her head. "My business is still shut down, and likely will be for another day," she said. "They passed us with flying colors, but, you know."

"Yeah," Ruthie said. "Bureaucracy. I wanted to leave this horrific place the second the guy passed out, but my company won't let me. No offense about the town."

"None taken," Maggie said, though the woman's words grated on her nerves. "Why can't you leave?"

"Because I work for the company that hosts these food eating events and they won't let me leave," she said. "We're tied up with the rest of the fair outfit and I can't just take off until they pull up stakes, too."

"What about the other guy? The second emcee," Maggie asked. "Is he an employee, too?"

Ruthie nodded her head. She turned to the side and coughed loudly. Her appearance suddenly shifted from an attractive middle-aged woman to a sixty-year-old smoker. "We all are, us, the judges, even some of the assistants," she said.

"Wait a moment," Maggie said. "Do you mean

that some of the assistants to the competitors work for your company as well?"

"Yeah," Ruthie said. She shrugged her shoulders like it wasn't a big deal. "They pay them minimum wage to stand behind those guys and help them dunk their hot dogs in water."

"What about the Flame Thrower contest?"

"Oh, those guys bring their own assistants along with them," Ruthie said. "Valiant doesn't mess with them any more than they have to."

"What's Valiant?" Maggie asked.

"Valiant Foods is the company that sponsors the food competitions," Ruthie continued. "They provide the setup, the food prep tent, even the food itself. But those pepper eaters, those guys are a different breed altogether."

"How are they different?" Maggie asked her. She turned and glanced over her shoulder at Ruby.

"Well, they live or die by this competition stuff." Ruthie shrugged. "I don't know how else to put it. The hot pepper eating contests are much more serious to those folks. You've got people who make this their full time job, while the hot dog eaters and others sometimes just show up for the heck of it. It's a fun way to spend their free time, and if they can take home a five hundred dollar prize at the end of the day, the stomachache is worth it."

"But the pepper eaters, they are different," Maggie said.

Ruthie nodded again. "Like I said, a lot of those folks make this their career of choice. The money is better, and the stakes are higher."

"Are the foods prepared in the same tent?" Maggie asked.

Ruthie shook her head. "No, the peppers are usually brought in from off site," she said. "That's one reason Valiant won't let us go just yet. I guess the coroner still has incomplete lab work or something on the peppers. It's a little harder when all of that stuff is done by a third party."

"A third party? Who prepares the peppers?" Maggie asked.

"Lady, are you writing a book or something?" Ruthie asked suddenly. "You sure do have a lot of questions. And no offense, but I am sick and tired of repeating myself over and over to every cop in the area. I already told them that the peppers usually come from a local grocery store or another outfit Valiant pays to set this stuff up. Either way, we don't even meet those people until we roll into a new place."

"So, there isn't a lot of reason to think they would have had anything to do with the death of the contestant?" Maggie said.

"Not really," Ruthie replied. She took her drinks from the serving window and turned to leave. "Listen, I'm glad they didn't try to pin this on you, but there is no reason to think anyone had it in for Virgil. He was a beloved member of the competition eating family. Nobody would have wanted him dead. All of this hullabaloo is going to wither away, and the truth will come out."

"What is the truth, Ruthie?" Maggie asked her as she walked away.

Ruthie stopped and turned back to her. "The truth is, eating like that decade after decade is bound to mess something up inside. And the faster these doctors and police officers can get that through their heads and leave that poor man to rest in peace, the better. Now, if you will excuse me, I have to go."

Maggie waited until the woman was far enough away to be out of earshot and then turned back to Ruby.

"Did you hear all of that?" she asked her.

"I heard enough," Ruby said. "I think it is pretty clear that the peppers were not the source of any poison."

Maggie sighed as they walked toward the donut truck. She felt the weight of the situation on her shoulders as they walked. She had no better idea what had happened than she had as she watched Virgil slump over in his plate.

CHAPTER TEN

After a brief check-in with Naomi and Bradley, Maggie and Ruby decided to head back to the truck. When she reached the passenger side, Maggie hesitated. "I think we should go to the Dogwood House," she announced.

"But what about what Albert said? I don't think he means for us to come back so soon," Ruby said.

"I don't think we ought to wait," Maggie said. She pulled her phone and fired off a quick text to Brett informing him where she was going.

"Okay, but be careful," he wrote back almost immediately. "Dr. Marsh just called me. They ruled out hot peppers as the cause of death."

"Brett just said that the peppers didn't cause Virgil's death," Maggie said aloud.

"Does she still think his death was deliberate? What caused the rupture?" Ruby asked.

Maggie texted the question to Brett and waited for his reply. "Definitely still murder. The question is what substance could have caused the rupture," he said.

"Still murder." Maggie said nothing more while they drove out of the fairground parking lot and headed toward the hills on the far side of the town of Dogwood Mountain.

Ruby pulled into the driveway and parked just as she had done over a half hour earlier. The two of them exited the truck and rushed up to the back porch of the large house. "Why are we in such a hurry?" Ruby whispered when Maggie reached for the door knob on the back door.

"I don't know," Maggie said. "But I have a feeling." She twisted the door knob slightly and smiled when she found it unlocked. Gently, she eased the door open and stepped inside the large kitchen.

"Gretchen?" Maggie called out her name when she walked a few more feet inside.

"Hang on a minute," Ruby whispered. "I think I hear something."

Maggie hesitated. She held her breath for a

moment and tried her best to listen. She could hear the sound of footsteps somewhere in the large house, and then a series of slamming doors. "It's on the third floor," she shouted and headed across the kitchen to the familiar hall.

Ruby followed close behind. Maggie made it to the first staircase and ran up a flight. "Gretchen," she called out.

"What are you doing here?" Amanda stepped directly in front of Maggie, blocking her from reaching the next set of stairs.

"What is going on upstairs?" Maggie asked.

"Answer my question first," Amanda said.

Maggie lunged to one side, but the younger woman was faster. "Did you have anything to do with killing your husband?" she blurted out.

"What did you say to me?" Amanda screamed. She moved toward Maggie. Her open hand landed a stinging blow on the side of Maggie's face.

Ruby closed the gap between herself and the two women and shoved Amanda backwards. She landed on the steps behind her. "You just committed assault," Ruby said. She stood between Maggie and the young blonde. "I think you better think long and hard before you make your next move. I don't know if you are aware of this, but this woman's significant other happens to be the county sheriff!"

Later, when Maggie asked her why she decided to spout off about her relationship with Brett, Ruby claimed temporary insanity. "I just wanted to scare her off of you," she said.

Amanda sat down on the third step and buried her head. "Look, I didn't do anything to my husband," she cried. "I know it seems like an open and shut case, but I did love him. We weren't married for the reasons you're assuming, just because he was close to thirty years older than me."

"You slapped me," Maggie stated, a little late. She rested her hand on her burning cheek.

"Please don't press charges against me," Amanda said. "I'm sorry that I slapped you. It's just been really rough since the competition. I can't leave this place until the cops say I can go. I can't even make the arrangements for my husband's funeral until they release me and him both." She covered her eyes and began to sob.

"Amanda, what is going on upstairs?" Ruby said at last. "We heard stomping and doors slamming."

"I don't know, but I think there is something going on upstairs with the owners and that couple,

Louis and Donna. They're having an argument," Amanda said.

"Do you know what they are fighting about?" Maggie asked her.

"Something the old man that takes care of this place found inside their room," Amanda said. "I heard the woman scream at him that he had no right to check their room."

"Get out!" The shout came from right above them. Amanda stood quickly and moved to the side. Maggie rushed up the stairs by her. Ruby followed closely behind.

They reached the top. Maggie looked up and down both hallways before she headed to her right. She rounded the L-shaped hall and stopped a few feet from the door to the bedroom at the end. Gretchen was slumped to the side in a chair situated in the hallway next to a bookcase.

"Ruby," Maggie said. Immediately Ruby rushed to the older woman's side. She picked up her hand and began patting it. The woman roused and cradled her head in her free hand.

"I don't feel so good," Gretchen said. "Those people have got something noxious in that room."

"It's okay, Miss Gretchen," Ruby said. "We're

going to call for some help and get you looked at." She reached for her phone and dialed quickly.

"Sit with her until the ambulance arrives," Maggie ordered Amanda. "Keep her alert and don't let her get up from that chair."

"Be careful," Gretchen said weakly. "I don't know what they have in there."

Ruby stood up and left the older woman to Amanda's care. Somehow Maggie knew Amanda was innocent of harming her husband, though the side of her cheek still smarted from the slap.

"What are we going to do?" Ruby whispered to her.

"I don't know, but we need to get in touch with Brooks and let him know there is a disturbance here." Ruby nodded and pulled her phone out again. Maggie watched as she dialed 9-1-1.

"I am not going to say it to you again," a woman's voice boomed across the hallway. "Get out of here! Leave or else!"

"Just calm down," a second voice said. Maggie was sure she was hearing the voice of Louis speaking to his wife, Donna. "Whatever that is, let's just take a deep breath and calm down."

Maggie glanced toward Ruby, hoping to communicate her intentions before she began to inch closer to the bedroom door. When she reached the end of the hallway, she stepped into the view of the room. She could see Donna on the far side of the room. She held a clear glass bottle in her hand. It was filled nearly to the top with a cloudy, transparent liquid. Louis, her husband, stood close to the foot of the bed, just ten feet from her. Albert was on the other side of the bed, straight across from Donna.

"You just stop right there," Donna shouted when she spotted her.

Maggie cleared her throat. "I don't know if you all are aware of this, but I think Gretchen might be in some trouble out here."

"Just get out of here, lady," Donna yelled.

"We have called for an ambulance," Maggie continued. She forced herself to stay calm and for her voice to remain even. "So, whatever you might have going on in here, it's best to just calmly walk away right now. Albert? Why don't you come on out here and let this couple pack their things. That way they can just walk down those stairs and get in their car and drive away. No harm, no foul."

"She has something in that glass," Albert said, pointing across the bed. "It made Gretchen ill."

Maggie's eyes began to sting. "Well," she said. "Maybe she does have something in there. So, just set it down on the floor and leave it be. Then the paramedics will know if there is something to it and they can treat her." She smiled her best smile at Donna. "And you two can just drive right out of here and head back to where you came from. The state line is less than an hour from here."

"She's right," Ruby said cautiously behind her. "Just set that bottle right down there on the table beside the bed. We'll take care of everything else."

"She has the burns," Albert said again. "I saw them when she had her breakfast this morning."

"What burns?" Louis asked. For the first time, Maggie was sure he was about clueless as the rest of them.

"Albert," Maggie said quietly. "I don't think it matters now. Let's just give them a wide berth to make their way out of here before anyone else gets hurt."

"She has chemical burns! On her palms," Albert said.

Outside the third-floor window, a siren wailed. Donna leaned over to look out the window. "The cops are here! I thought you just called the medics!"

"It's probably our friend, Brooks," Ruby said

quickly. "You see, we're all a close family around here. Miss Gretchen out there in the hall? She is a close friend of ours, too. The cop in that car is probably only here because he's worried about her. You can just walk right out of here. Easy peasy."

Maggie heard the sound of the doors slamming open downstairs and the boots running up the first flight of stairs. Out of the corner of her eye, she saw the paramedics stop and stoop down next to Gretchen's chair.

"Please, Donna," Maggie whispered when she turned her attention back to the room. "Just set down that bottle and walk right on out of here."

"Please, honey," Louis said.

"Fine," Albert said, dropping his hands to his side. "Just go."

Donna stared at the doorway, then turned back to her husband. "Fine," she said at last. "Let's just walk out of here. There is nothing we need to take with us."

But Maggie heard another set of footsteps coming down the hall. She could see the blue uniform of the Dogwood Mountain Police Department begin to fill the hallway.

Donna appeared to notice the uniform, too. She shifted the bottle from her left to her right hand. She turned to the side and launched the glass container into the air. The liquid inside was thicker than Maggie guessed.

The liquid moved faster than the glass. Maggie watched as it escaped the bottle and bathed Albert's face. Immediately, he grabbed his face, screamed, and fell to his knees writhing in pain.

CHAPTER ELEVEN

Maggie rode along in the front of Ruby's truck as they followed behind the ambulance. Albert was taken in first. A second ambulance had been called for Gretchen, but more as a precaution than an emergency.

Albert, however, was in far worse shape. The first team of paramedics had rushed to his side. Maggie had to turn away while they removed his hands from his face. One forced him to the ground while the other began to cut the shirt away from his neck and shoulders. His skin beneath the clothing had already begun to blister and turned the darkest shade of red Maggie had ever seen on a human being.

With each touch, Albert screeched in pain. Before she knew what was happening, Brooks had her by the arm, leading her away from the bedroom and back down the hall toward the stairs.

"I wonder if he can survive that," Maggie blurted out suddenly. She turned to her best friend. "I mean, don't they have that math problem?"

"Math problem?" Ruby repeated.

"You know, how they determine whether or not a burn victim has any chance to live," Maggie said. "It's something like their age and the percentage of their body that was burned divided by the degree of the burns. Something like that."

"I think it's the age plus the area of the body burned," Ruby said.

Maggie was quiet for a long moment. "How old do you think Albert is?" she asked.

"Maggie, don't," Ruby said. "If he is too old, he won't make it. But whatever that liquid was, as long as it didn't go down his throat or burn his airways, he has a fighting chance. Let's just leave it at that."

Brett had arrived at the hospital before them. Maggie forced herself to hold back when she spotted him, though she was desperately tempted to run and bury her face in his chest, but he was there in an official capacity, taking witness statements from the police officers and the paramedics who witnessed the actions of Donna.

Louis was on his way to the county jail in the back of Brook's police cruiser. Donna had been transported in a third ambulance to another hospital. Maggie assumed that she would be under arrest as soon as she received treatment for the chemical burns on her hands.

Maggie followed Ruby to the waiting room where they sat for over an hour until Brett joined them. "Can the two of you tell me what happened?"

"We met the first emcee from the food competition at the fair," Ruby offered. "Maggie had a conversation with her, and we realized that there was no way anyone could have sabotaged the peppers."

"That was about the same time you texted me that the peppers had been ruled out," Maggie added.

"After that, we decided to go over to the Dogwood House," Ruby said. "When we got there, we let ourselves inside and heard noise upstairs. That's when we both headed up the steps to see what was going on."

"How did you get the shiner?" Brett asked Maggie. Her hand moved to her face again. Her skin was still hot to the touch.

"I had a very animated conversation with Amanda on the steps on the second floor," she said. "But I don't want to do anything about it."

"You don't want to press charges?"

Maggie shook her head. "She didn't kill her husband," she said.

"No, she didn't," Brett confirmed. "Donna did and we are prepared to charge her with his murder."

"Why did she do it?" Ruby asked. "That was drain cleaner or something in the glass bottle, wasn't it? The smell in that room after Donna threw it at Albert was overwhelming."

Brett nodded his head. "It was," he said. "And I would lay money down that Dr. Marsh is going to find residue of it in one of the cups from the food competition."

"But why?" Maggie said. "Why kill him? Why him?"

"We don't know that, not just yet," Brett said. "It's still possible that Virgil wasn't her intended target."

"Then, who was it?" Ruby asked.

"Louis," Brooks said. He walked through the waiting room doorway and took a seat across from Brett. "At least, that's the theory I am working with."

"Did he say something to you on the way to the jail?" Brett asked.

"Not much, but he was crying on the way," Brooks said. "I heard him say that he should have dropped out of the competition and that he didn't mean to drive his wife over the edge."

"She told me that she had been forced to leave competition eating because of her ulcers," Maggie said. "Maybe she was angry with him that he didn't quit when she had to. I bet she put the drain cleaner in the cup for Louis, but he was disqualified before he was able to drink any. Then Virgil, not paying attention in the moment, grabbed the wrong cup."

"I guess we will find out soon enough," Brooks said. "But it sounds like you're right on track."

"One way or the other, I've decided that I don't like watching people eat," Maggie said. "And I'm never eating anything spicy again."

CHAPTER TWELVE

Maggie closed her eyes and rested her head against the back of her chair for the second time in several long days. She could feel the crisp night air against her cheeks. The warmth of the bonfire wafted over her bare feet. She had pulled her feet out of her sandals and curled up in the large wooden chair.

Brett's hand rested on her arm. She turned to him and opened her eyes. "I can't believe you asked me that earlier," she said and rolled her eyes for the umpteenth time that evening.

"Are you ever going to let me live that down?" He shook his head and grinned.

"What did you do, young man?" Orson asked the sheriff. "You look like the cat that just ate a mouse."

"I made a mistake when I asked this beautiful lady out for dinner," Brett said.

"What did you do, ask her to go out for tacos or something?" Brooks asked from the other side of the fire pit. He looked down at his sleeping infant daughter.

"Yeah, because after the week she had, asking her to go eat in a restaurant serving hot peppers is a grand idea," Myra said. She winked at Maggie.

Brett hung his head a little further.

"Wait a minute," Orson said. He pointed his long finger in Brett's direction. "You honestly did that? You made a date with this lady to a Mexican restaurant after she watched a man die on a platter of hot peppers?"

"Technically, that isn't what he died from," Brett said, trying to give himself the benefit of the doubt.

"I don't think you can be saved by a technicality this time," Brooks joked.

Ruby was quiet for a moment, then began to shake her head. She covered her eyes with one hand and cleared her throat. "Sometimes I wonder how you manage to tie your shoes every morning, Brett Mission," she said. "Let alone run an entire sheriff's department."

"Not to mention how he keeps this lady in love with him," Orson muttered. "Who asks a woman out to eat dinner in a place where they serve the same sort of food she just saw kill a man."

"Again, I'll remind you that it was not the peppers that killed him," Brett argued.

"Well, I haven't heard of many places with a tall, cool glass of drain cleaner on the menu, have you?" Orson shot back. "It's common sense that she would still associate the hot peppers with the memory."

"I hate to ask this, but what was his second suggestion?" Brooks teased. "Hot dogs soaked in water?"

Laughter rippled over the small gathering. Maggie wound her fingers in Brett's and squeezed. "No, you guys. Be nice," she said with a sideways glance at him. "He did ask me if I was in the mood for donuts, though."

"I did not," Brett sat upright in his chair and shouted. He dropped Maggie's hand and stood up. "You all are terrible, awful friends. I can't believe I'm sitting out here spending this beautiful night with any of you." He walked toward the outdoor cooler and plucked a beer bottle from the ice. When he returned to his seat, he was smiling and shaking his head.

"On a more serious note, do you think Louis will end up serving time along with his wife?" Naomi asked from her seat next to Ruby.

"That is going to depend on the prosecutor and whether or not they can prove that he had any prior knowledge of her plans," Brett said.

"What do you think, Sheriff?" Brooks asked him. "Innocent or guilty?"

Brett tipped the bottle to his lips and took a long drink. "It's hard to say, but it doesn't look good that he won't talk," he said. "It doesn't make a man innocent or guilty but refusing to answer basic questions is not a good look. We did find out Donna's plans were just like Maggie said. She was after her husband, but Virgil ended up being the victim."

Maggie was proud of herself for getting it right but tried not to let on. "I think Louis seemed a little dumbfounded when we pointed out the drain cleaner his wife had been keeping in their room. I would almost guess that he didn't know what she had done."

"He did seem as shocked as the rest of us," Ruby added.

"Is there any word on how old Albert is doing?" Myra asked.

"Albert will be released from the hospital in a few

days or so," Orson announced. "And when he is, he owes me a game of chess."

All eyes turned to Orson. Maggie glanced at Ruby, then turned back to the old man. "Orson, have you been to see Albert in the hospital?"

"Have any of you? I haven't heard a single one of you take up the cross to go and check in on the old man," Orson grumbled.

"Yeah, but, Orson," Brooks began. "We all thought you sort of hated Albert."

"Why would I hate him? That's a huge conclusion for you all to jump to," Orson said. "And since you asked, the drain cleaner missed the most vital parts. His airways and his esophagus were cleared. His eyes weren't burned. He is a lucky man. He will have some scarring, but no disabling injuries."

"We all thought you were jealous of him living there and working so close to Gretchen," Myra said.

Orson shifted in his seat. He frowned and folded his arms. "No man like Albert Boudreaux is going to keep me from seeing any woman," he muttered. "Besides, the man cheats at chess. No woman in their right mind would be okay with that."

The chuckling began slowly. Soon, laughter erupted from almost every seat around the circle.

Maggie wiped the tears from her eyes and buried her head in Brett's shoulder. "Oh, Orson," she said. "I needed that."

If you enjoyed Donut You Dare, check out the next book in the series, Glaze of Glory, today!

AUTHOR'S NOTE

I'd love to hear your thoughts on my books, the storylines, and anything else that you'd like to comment on—reader feedback is very important to me. My contact information, along with some other helpful links, is listed on the next page. If you'd like to be on my list of "folks to contact" with updates, release and sales notifications, etc.... just shoot me an email and let me know. Thanks for reading!

Also…

… if you're looking for more great reads, Summer Prescott Books publishes several popular series by outstanding Cozy Mystery authors.

CONTACT SUMMER PRESCOTT
BOOKS PUBLISHING

Blog and Book Catalog: http://summerprescottbooks.com

Email: summer.prescott.cozies@gmail.com

And…be sure to check out the Summer Prescott Cozy Mysteries fan page and Summer Prescott Books Publishing Page on Facebook – let's be friends!

To sign up for our fun and exciting newsletter, which will give you opportunities to win prizes and swag, enter contests, and be the first to know about New Releases, click here: http://summerprescottbooks.com

Made in United States
North Haven, CT
15 March 2023

34102861R00065